To Mary and Jonathan
Merry Christmas
from the S.S. Happiness crew.

Jane Dutton

12/25/82

The Third Adventure of the S.S. Happiness Crew:

CAP'N JOSHUA'S SUPER SECRET

By June Dutton

Illustrations by Eric Hill

Determined Productions, Inc.
San Francisco

Other books in the S.S. Happiness Crew series
by June Dutton, illustrated by Eric Hill:

The First Adventure of the S.S. Happiness Crew:
Cap'n Joshua's Dangerous Dilemma.

The Second Adventure of the S.S. Happiness Crew:
Mystery in the Middle of the Ocean.

Published by Determined Productions, Inc., San Francisco, California
Printed in Hong Kong
Library of Congress Card Catalog No. 82-71287
ISBN: 0-915696-50-9

Cap'n Joshua seems sad. Christmas is almost here and he is lonesome for his wife and two children. He doesn't like being away from home at Christmas. But when you are the captain of a big ship, you must go wherever your ship goes.

Josh sighs and thinks, I must forget about being lonesome. I'll find Tasha and see if everything is ready for our Christmas Eve party.

1

Tasha is in the ship library with her friend Allie. "Hello, Cap'n Joshua. Allie and I have been talking about the Christmas tree. We're going to trim it tomorrow. Are you going to help?"

"I wouldn't miss it, Tasha. I've seen Chef Jambon making all those delicious treats to hang on our tree and I want to be in on the fun. Let's go to the kitchen and see if everything is ready for tomorrow. I want this to be a very merry Christmas for everyone aboard the *S.S. Happiness*."

"Welcome to my Christmas kitchen," says Chef Jambon. "Things are in a mess, Cap'n Joshua, but don't worry, everything will be ready for the tree trimming tomorrow. Have you seen Velvetino? He promised to help with the cranberry strings, but he's disappeared."

4

"I'll string cranberries," offers Allie. "I do it every year at home. You won't even have to show me how."

"That would be a great help," says Jambon smiling. "The *S.S. Happiness* tree is pretty big. I know I have made enough cookies and candy canes and popcorn balls, but we need more cranberry strings. Velvetino better get back here...I'm very cross with him!"

Just then Velvetino bursts through the doorway sobbing, "IT'S TERRIBLE…TERRIBLE… TERRIBLE! WHAT ARE WE GOING TO DO ABOUT CHRISTMAS?"

Startled, Chef Jambon drops his bowl of cranberries, scattering them all over the kitchen.

"Something AWFUL has happened," cries Velvetino, who is so upset he doesn't see how annoyed Jambon is.

"Stop your babbling this minute," orders the chef. "Stand still and tell us what's wrong. Then pick up my cranberries—every one of them."

"IT'S RUINED! I SAW IT AND IT'S RUINED! COME AND LOOK! SEE FOR YOURSELF." He bursts back out the door.

Everyone runs after Velvetino, squashing cranberries as they go. Jambon shouts, "STOP, VELVETINO! STOP IMMEDIATELY! What IS the matter with you?"

Velvetino scurries out on deck, sees Jack and waves for him to follow him.

"Where are you going in such a hurry?" shouts Dr. Phineas as the parade rushes past his office.

"I don't know," hollers Jack. "Come along and find out."

They clatter down one stairway after another. "You're making more noise than my whole engine room," shouts Wrecker as they pass his door. "What's going on?"

"Come with us and find out," cries Jack.

At last Velvetino stops in front of the doorway to the storeroom. "See there," he squeaks. "I told you it was ruined!"

"Oh, you are right," groans Tasha. "Our beautiful Christmas tree IS ruined. How can we have Christmas without a Christmas tree?"

"WHAT A DISASTER!" gasps Cap'n Joshua. "A barrel of ship's paint has spilled all over our tree."

"Do you think we can fix it?" asks Allie unhappily.

"I don't think so," says Dr. Phineas. "Too much paint."

Jack and Wrecker shake their heads sadly.

"Come now, let's not be so gloomy," says Cap'n Josh. "We can't let this spoil our Christmas. I'll think of SOMETHING!"

But before Cap'n Josh has a moment to think, Velvetino squeaks, "I know what… we'll MAKE a tree. We can build it out of pipes and wires from Wrecker's engine room and from anything else we can find on the ship. We can paint it green. And when we decorate it with Chef Jambon's cookies and candy and popcorn and cranberries, it will be beautiful."

12

Tasha isn't pleased with the idea. But Jambon nods and smiles at his little helper. "That's a fine idea, Velvetino. I'm proud of you...I'm not cross anymore."

Cap'n Josh nods and smiles, too. He's thought of an even better idea—but he decides to keep it a secret until he is sure his idea will work.

The next morning as she comes out on deck Tasha stops Jack. "Have you seen Allie? I have something EXCITING to tell her."

"Oh, Tasha," he says, "TELL ME, FIRST. I love exciting news more than anyone. Is it about Christmas?"

"Wait a minute, Jack. Let's find Allie...then I'll tell both of you."

Allie is just finishing her breakfast as Tasha and Jack come looking for her in the dining room. "I wish I could make scrambled eggs as good as yours," she says, smiling at Chef Jambon. "How do you do it? What's your secret?"

"What's that? ANOTHER SECRET?" cries Tasha. "Does Jambon have a secret, too?"

"What are you so EXCITED about, Tasha? Chef Jambon and I are talking about scrambled eggs. What's all this about SECRETS?"

15

Out of the corner of his eye Jambon is watching Velvetino stack dirty dishes on a tray. The pile is dangerously high—ready to topple.

"Tell us quickly, Tasha," says Jambon, looking nervously at the tower of plates. "I have lots to do before our Christmas Eve party."

"We—ll," whispers Tasha, "I think Cap'n Joshua has a secret. I want all of you to help me find out what it is."

"I'll help," says Jack, raising his hand. "But I think we should tell Dr. Phineas and Wrecker, too. The more brains we put to work, the sooner we'll find out what Cap'n Josh's secret is. Let's tell Sir Rex, too. He's a REAL detective."

"Just a minute," Allie says. "What makes you so sure Cap'n Joshua has a secret?"

"Because," Tasha whispers mysteriously, "he called me to his cabin a while ago, but he wasn't there. Then as I was leaving he rushed in and apologized because he was delayed in the radio room. He mumbled something about Christmas being a busy time of year.

"I asked if he got a radio message about Christmas. He shook his head and said absolutely not, but I'm not so sure. He was excited, and his eyes twinkled more than usual.

"Then he asked about our plans for the Christmas tree. I told him I was worried about having it ready in time for the party. He said not to worry because he's sure we'll have a tree in time." Tasha sighs. "I wish I was as sure. The only thing I'M sure of is that Cap'n Joshua has a SECRET!"

Allie frowns.

"Strange. He MUST have gotten a message. I wonder what it was. Do you think anything is WRONG aboard the *S.S. Happiness?* Has anyone noticed anything?"

They all shake their heads except Chef Jambon. He's trotting off to save his precious plates from falling on Velvetino's foolish head.

19

"If there is anything wrong," says Jack, "Cap'n Joshua would tell us. We are his crew—he knows he can depend on us. Let's ask him if everything is OK."

They look for Cap'n Josh in his cabin, but he's not there. He's not on the bridge, in the wheelhouse or in the engine room.

"Let's try the radio room," suggests Allie. "I bet THAT'S where he is."

Sure enough! Cap'n Josh is just coming out of the radio room. He's smiling happily. "Good morning, Captain," says Jack. "It looks like you had some good news—anything you want to tell us?"

"No time now, Jack. I thought everyone was busy putting together a Christmas tree—better get at it—there's not much time." He walks off, chuckling.

"He's not going to tell us his secret," says Jack, smiling. "But I'm sure it's a GOOD secret. Cap'n Joshua wouldn't look so pleased if it were a BAD secret."

21

The next day Tasha, Allie, Jack, Dr. Phineas, Sir Rex and Velvetino are standing with Wrecker in his engine room looking at a big drawing tacked to the wall.

"Do you really think we can build a Christmas tree like that?" asks Dr. Phineas. It looks quite difficult—even for a clever doctor like me."

"It's a crazy Christmas tree," laughs Jack.

"I don't like crazy Christmas trees," says Tasha unhappily. "I'd much rather have a REAL one."

"Don't pout, Tasha," Sir Rex scolds. "If we don't get on with the job you won't have ANY tree."

The engine phone rings. "Yes, Cap'n Josh…right away… we'll hurry."

Wrecker hangs up the phone and cries, "LET'S GO! Captain Josh wants everyone on deck. He has a SURPRISE for the whole ship."

"I knew it! I knew it!" Tasha squeals. "I told you! I told you!"

They run up the stairs two at a time and hurry out on deck.

"Do you really think Cap'n Joshua is going to tell us his secret?"
asks Dr. Phineas.

"Of course he is," answers Tasha.

"Sh-h!" Allie frowns. "Listen to the captain!"

"I HAVE A CHRISTMAS SURPRISE FOR THE *S.S. HAPPINESS*. LOOK OUT THERE." Cap'n Joshua points to a tiny black dot in the sky far out over the ocean. "NOW WATCH…WATCH VERY CAREFULLY!"

The dot grows bigger and bigger. Jack shouts, "IT'S AN AIRPLANE!"

"Yes…a very SPECIAL airplane," cries Cap'n Joshua. "Keep watching."

Soon the plane zooms low over the *S.S. Happiness*, turns and zooms over again. The third time it zooms over it drops a parachute that floats slowly down to the deck. The crowd shouts. "HOORAY...HOORAY...HOORAY!"

"MERRY CHRISTMAS! MERRY CHRISTMAS!" cries Tasha. "So this was your secret, Cap'n Josh. What a wonderful surprise!" She throws her arms around him and laughs merrily.

"Now you won't have any more secrets to talk about, Tasha," says the Captain. He looks at Wrecker and winks. "I'm glad of that!" says Tasha. "We have no more time for secrets. We will be too busy decorating our beautiful tree."

"Be careful up there, Tasha!" warns Cap'n Joshua.

"Keep the ladder steady, Velvetino," says Dr. Phineas. "Tasha doesn't want a broken leg for Christmas. She couldn't dance at the party."

30

In rushes Jack. "Cap'n Joshua," he says, "they want you in the radio room. AN URGENT MESSAGE!"

The Captain looks worried. "I hope nothing has gone wrong with my plan," he mumbles.

Jack perks up his ears. "What's that? WHAT PLAN?"

Cap'n Joshua frowns and hurries off without answering.

Pointing at the Christmas tree, Jack says, "I don't think THIS was Cap'n Joshua's only secret. I bet he has another secret... one that is even BIGGER and BETTER than this."

"Ooh—oo, goody," squeaks Velvetino. "More secrets, more surprises."

He is so delighted he lets go of the ladder, claps his hands and does a little dance.

Tasha almost tumbles.

"Let's not get too excited," Allie says. "If Cap'n Joshua has another secret, he will tell us soon enough. In the meantime we must finish trimming the tree. REMEMBER—tomorrow is Christmas Eve."

33

Next morning, Cap'n Josh is up early. He is standing on the ship's bridge looking through his binoculars. He turns 'round and 'round looking in all directions. The sea is calm.

"My plan should work perfectly," he says.

He walks back and forth. He can't stand still. He is too excited. He decides to go to the engine room and talk to Wrecker. (He has already told Wrecker his plan because he needs him to help. Josh is glad Wrecker can keep a secret.)

"Cheerio, Captain, you look especially happy this morning. Are you planning another jolly surprise for us?"

Sir Rex is enjoying a morning stroll with his friend Lola.

"Perhaps you are going to make it snow for Christmas. That WOULD be a surprise, indeed."

"I don't think I can do that, Sir Rex," chuckles Cap'n Josh, "but I think we will have a very merry Christmas anyway."

He salutes and hurries off to the engine room.

"This is for Cap'n Joshua, Allie," Tasha says. "Guess what it is?" Tasha is tying a big bow on a package. "You get three guesses."

"It's not a tie…wrong shape," Allie laughs. "I don't think it's an umbrella. How about a bicycle?"

"Stop kidding me, Allie. Make a real guess. I'll give you a hint. You can't eat it or wear it or return it."

"H'm—m." Allie frowns and thinks hard. "No use, Tasha. I give up. What is it?"

"DANCING LESSONS," squeals Tasha. "I'm going to teach Cap'n Josh to DANCE…he's not very good."

"He'll like that, Tasha. Dancing lessons are more fun than a tie or an unbrella."

"But not more fun than a BICYCLE," squeaks Velvetino.

36

Tasha has just put her gift under the tree when
Cap'n Joshua comes in. He smiles.

"Our Christmas tree is
the prettiest I have ever seen,"
he says. "I want everything to be
PERFECT tonight. This is going to
be a VERY SPECIAL Christmas Eve."

"Christmas Eve is ALWAYS special,"
Allie says. "Is tonight going to be more
special than usual?"

"I hope so!" Cap'n Joshua smiles mysteriously and
hurries off before he has to answer any more questions.

"I KNOW IT...I JUST KNOW IT," cries Tasha. "He has another
secret...and we are going to find out what it is tonight."

37

On his way to the engine room Cap'n Josh runs into Jack.

"Merry Christmas, Cap'n Josh!"

"Same to you," answers Josh. Then he whispers, "Jack, I want you to make an announcement over the intercom just before dinner. Ask everyone aboard the *S.S. Happiness* to be on deck at midnight. Don't ask questions...just do as I say!"

"Aye, aye, Captain." Jack salutes. Josh hurries on.

"Did you hear THAT, Allie?"

"You were right, Tasha. Cap'n Joshua IS going to tell us his secret tonight. I can't wait."

It's something SPECIAL…you can be sure of that, Allie."

"Did you hear THAT, Wrecker? What is Cap'n Josh up to?" asks Dr. Phineas.

"Something SPECIAL…you can be sure of that," answers Wrecker. (He wishes he could tell Dr. Phineas about Cap'n Joshua's plan. But he promised not to tell anyone…so he won't.)

ATTENTION EVERYONE...

"Did you hear THAT?" squeaks Velvetino.

"Of course I did," answers Chef Jambon. "It sounds like Cap'n Joshua has another surprise for us, something very SPECIAL, I bet."

The whole ship is buzzing with excitement.

"I've never had a more exciting Christmas," Lola says to Sir Rex. "I wonder what Cap'n Joshua is planning now."

"I expect we shall just have to be patient and wait for midnight," says Sir Rex. "I rather think we are in for some grand excitement."

40

Close to midnight, Josh looks at his watch. Time to go," he says. "I hope nothing goes wrong with my plan. Wrecker is doing his job— the ship is slowing down."

Everyone cheers and shouts as Cap'n Joshua comes on deck.

"MERRY CHRISTMAS, CAP'N JOSHUA!"

"MERRY CHRISTMAS TO EVERYONE," he shouts back.

The crowd is so excited that no one seems to notice the ship has stopped. Cap'n Josh is pleased that Wrecker is following his orders so perfectly.

"JACK!" Cap'n Josh points into the darkness. "TURN ON THE SPOTLIGHT...SHINE IT OUT THERE!"

No one says a word. Then Tasha whispers, "What's out there?"

"I can't see anything," Allie whispers back.

All at once there are shouts. "LOOK...LOOK THERE, DO YOU SEE WHAT I SEE? WHAT IS IT, A WHALE? I CAN'T BELIEVE IT. IT'S A..."

"A SUBMARINE," cries Cap'n Josh, "a submarine with a VERY IMPORTANT PASSENGER."

"THREE CHEERS FOR CAP'N JOSHUA!"

"MERRY CHRISTMAS TO ALL," cries Cap'n Josh. "Let's help Santa Claus aboard!"

42

CHRISTMAS HAS COME TO THE S.S. HAPPINESS!

JOIN THE S.S. HAPPINESS
CREW CLUB!
To receive your official pin,
write to:
Tasha Elephant, President
S.S. HAPPINESS
CREW CLUB
c/o The Happiness Shop
Box 2150, San Francisco,
CA 94126